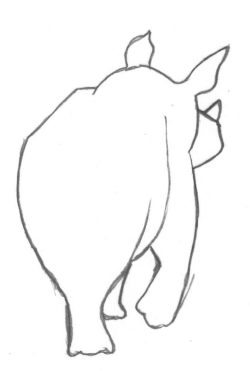

A NOTE ABOUT THE ILLUSTRATIONS

When I was illustrating this book, the words I used on the buildings and animals came from several sources. These were random snippets of advertising slogans, and short phrases from famous environmental speeches made by Martin Luther King, Chief Seattle and Paul Hawken, plus a few of my own, translated into many different languages. My aim was to contrast the bleakness of advertising with inspirational words such as these from Paul Hawken:

Forget that this task of planet-saving is not possible in the time required. Don't be put off by people who know what is not possible. Do what needs to be done, and check to see if it was impossible only after you are done.

I believe that the world can change for the better, but it will change one heart at a time. Change your heart, change the world.

Nicola Davies

For Mary, who always said I should
For Jackie, Cathy, and Petr who said I could
and for Dan who said I would, even when I thought I wouldn't.

N.D.

#TinyOwlLast

Copyright © Tiny Owl Publishing 2020
Text and illustrations © Nicola Davies 2020

Nicola Davies has asserted her right under the Copyright, Designs
and Patents Act 1988 to be identified as Author and Illustrator of this work
First published in the UK in 2020 and in the US in 2020 by Tiny Owl Publishing, London
www.tinyowl.co.uk

A catalogue record for this book is available from the British Library.
CIP record of this book is available from the Library of Congress

UK ISBN 978-1-910328-48-4
US ISBN 978-1-910328-64-4

Printed in China

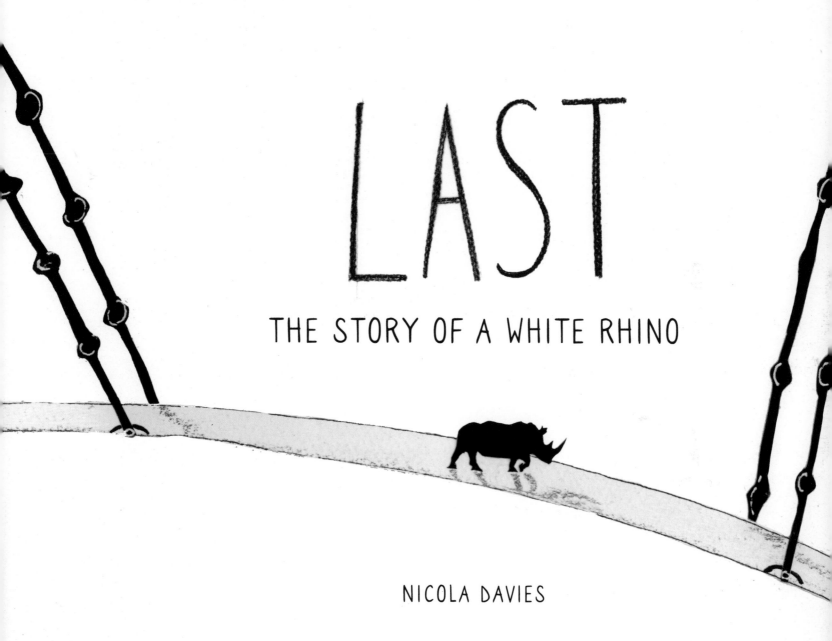

LAST

THE STORY OF A WHITE RHINO

NICOLA DAVIES

TINY OWL

I am the last.

... can change one heart at a time. Change your heart and change ...

...の心を変えること...

Faodaidh an saoghal aon chridhe atharrachadl ...o chridhe agus atharraich an saoghal

心を変えることができます

Ο κόσμος μπορεί να αλλάξει μία καρδια κάθε

I've looked and looked,
but I've never found
another like me.

Long ago in the old place,
        there were others.

Big ones fighting, little ones playing.

And there was mama.
Mama!

I followed her through
the grass and flowers.

And stayed close
in the darkness.

She smelled beautiful.

But one day she fell down
and lay still, so still.

I was taken
in a box.

When the box opened, I was here.

There was no smell of grass or flowers.

Even the rain smelled empty.

I am not the only last.

There are many
lasts here.

We look.
We pace.

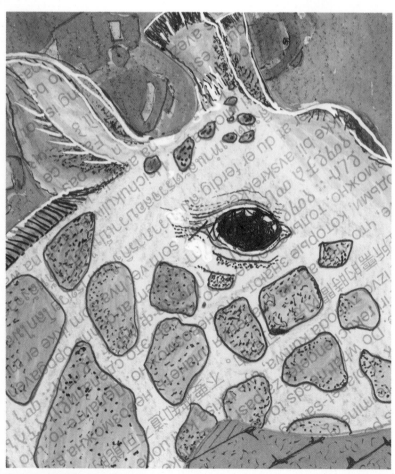

We lie down, and close our eyes.

Where are the others for us?

What has happened to the world?

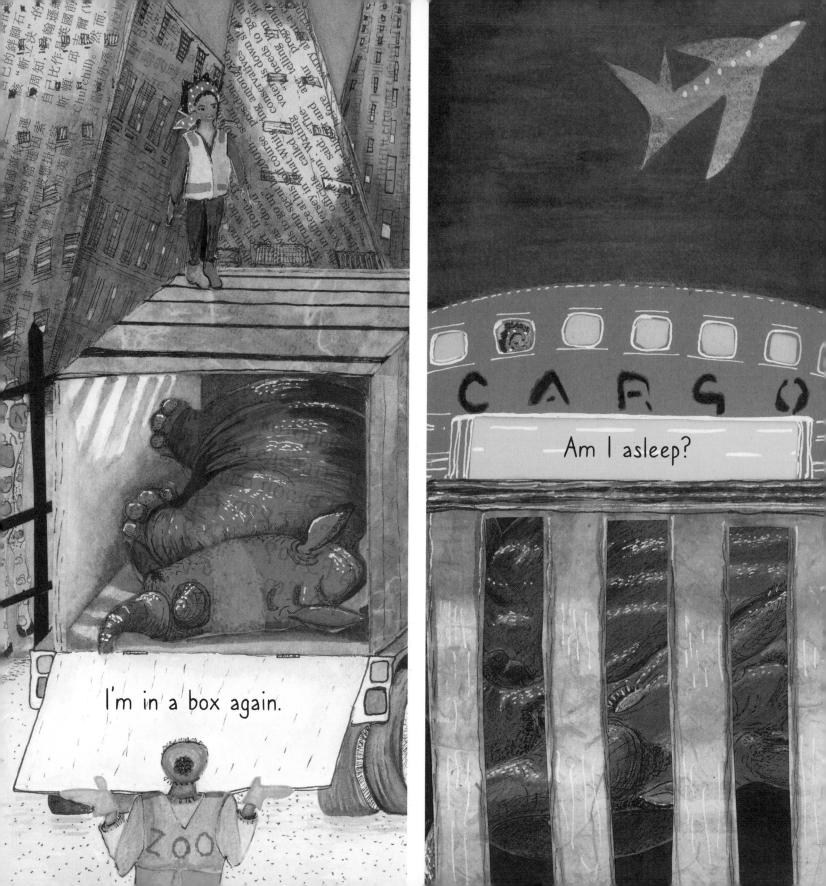

No, I'm awake and I smell grass
and earth and real fat rain.

It is the old place!
And there is another....

She is not mama.
But she smells beautiful.

Perhaps we are not the last after all.

THE STORY OF SUDAN THE RHINO

This book was inspired by the true story of a real rhino named Sudan. Rhinos were once plentiful in Africa, Asia, and even in Europe. But when Sudan was born, members of his subspecies, the Northern White Rhino, had been hunted almost to extinction for their horn. Rhinos' horn is made of the same material as your nails. Yet, some humans believe it has magical healing properties. Thousands of rhinos have been killed for their horn.

In an attempt to save Northern White Rhinos from extinction, Sudan was captured aged two, in 1975 with five other rhinos and taken to a zoo in the Czech Republic. Five years later, all the Northern White Rhinos in the wild had been killed. And although Sudan did become a father when he grew up, few of his children survived, and his species was in big trouble.

In 2009 Sudan and two other rhinos were returned to Africa in the hope that they would breed more successfully there. Armed guards were with them 24 hours a day to protect them from poachers. But despite the best of care, no baby rhinos were born, and in March 2018, Sudan, the very last male Northern White Rhino, died, leaving just two elderly females. When they die Northern White Rhinos will be extinct.

Yet the story of rhinos is not over. Sudan's closest relatives are Southern White Rhinos. There are more than 10,000 Southern White rhinos in the wild, and over 700 in captivity. Around the world there are four other rhino species. All of them are still threatened by illegal hunting for their horn, and they face threats from habitat destruction and climate change. But wildlife rangers, scientists, and conservationists are working hard to protect rhinos and to make sure they have a future. You can help by telling people about rhinos and how special they are, and by supporting wildlife charities.

Sudan himself may still have a part to play. His sperm have been frozen and could be used to make a Southern White Rhino female pregnant. So Sudan junior could perhaps bring Northern White rhinos back into the world.

Nicola Davies

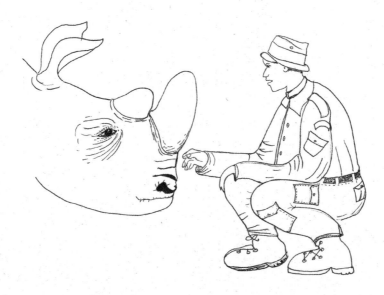